Purchase other books in this series:
Quantum Leaps in Princeton's Place
Six Doors Down

THE FUTURE *is* MY PAST

... THE END OF A TRILOGY

DR. DONNA CLOVIS

BALBOA PRESS
A DIVISION OF HAY HOUSE

Copyright © 2017 Dr. Donna Clovis.
Author Credits: Award-winning journalist

All rights reserved. No part of this book may be used or reproduced by any means, graphic, electronic, or mechanical, including photocopying, recording, taping or by any information storage retrieval system without the written permission of the author except in the case of brief quotations embodied in critical articles and reviews.

Balboa Press books may be ordered through booksellers or by contacting:

Balboa Press
A Division of Hay House
1663 Liberty Drive
Bloomington, IN 47403
www.balboapress.com
1 (877) 407-4847

Because of the dynamic nature of the Internet, any web addresses or links contained in this book may have changed since publication and may no longer be valid. The views expressed in this work are solely those of the author and do not necessarily reflect the views of the publisher, and the publisher hereby disclaims any responsibility for them.

The author of this book does not dispense medical advice or prescribe the use of any technique as a form of treatment for physical, emotional, or medical problems without the advice of a physician, either directly or indirectly. The intent of the author is only to offer information of a general nature to help you in your quest for emotional and spiritual well-being. In the event you use any of the information in this book for yourself, which is your constitutional right, the author and the publisher assume no responsibility for your actions.

This is a work of fiction. All of the characters, names, incidents, organizations, and dialogue in this novel are either the products of the author's imagination or are used fictitiously.

Any people depicted in stock imagery provided by Thinkstock are models, and such images are being used for illustrative purposes only.
Certain stock imagery © Thinkstock.

Print information available on the last page.

ISBN: 978-1-5043-8490-2 (sc)
ISBN: 978-1-5043-8492-6 (hc)
ISBN: 978-1-5043-8491-9 (e)

Library of Congress Control Number: 2017911754

Balboa Press rev. date: 08/10/2017

This book is dedicated to my loving husband, Jim,
my parents, my in-laws, and my children—
the past, the present, and the future of my lifetime.

And thank you always to my editor, Gabriella Oldham

The voiceless have a voice. A journalist's job is to amplify it.
        -- the late Steve Buttry, journalist (May 18, 2016)

I sit in Einstein's lecture hall at Princeton University and write on a regular basis. The warmth of the sun coming through the window speckles my brown skin. I follow footsteps of ideas and thoughts that I hear in the silence of synchronicity. It is like sitting in the Rosedale House of *Quantum Leaps in Princeton's Place*. My body and mind are in space at the right time. And then I walk down the path to take my courses in theoretical and quantum physics…

This is my journey…

Contents

Introduction		xi
Foreword	The Conscious as Quantum	xv
Chapter 1	A Mad Hatter's Tea Party	1
Chapter 2	Down the Rabbit Hole	3
Chapter 3	Golden Afternoons at Princeton University	5
Chapter 4	The Cheshire Cat	7
Chapter 5	It's All About Time	9
Chapter 6	Heaven in a Hoagie	11
Chapter 7	Black Squirrels and Tiger Tales	13
Chapter 8	Pink	15
Chapter 9	Taking to Twitter	17
Chapter 10	Airports, Attorneys, and Other Explanations of Time Travel	18
Chapter 11	The Pool of Tears	20
Chapter 12	Lessons From a Caterpillar	23
Chapter 13	The Heart-Shaped Pin	27
Chapter 14	Bless "Said" Be the Peace Makers	30
Chapter 15	Tweets and Leaks, Fake News, Oh, My!	32
Chapter 16	Princeton: A Sanctuary City	34
Chapter 17	This Is Not America	36
Chapter 18	The Case of Woodrow Wilson Revisited	39
Chapter 19	Lights, Camera, Action!	41

Chapter 20	There's No Place Like Home	43
Chapter 21	Sacred Secrets	45
Chapter 22	A Mathematical Constant	47
Chapter 23	Who Stole the Art of News?	49
Chapter 24	The Freedom to Write: A Journalist's Story	51
Chapter 25	The Charter School Quadrille	53
Chapter 26	The Snow Queen's Ballet Grounds	55
Chapter 27	Stealing Time	57
Chapter 28	Theories of Racial Relativity Hidden in a House	59
Chapter 29	PJ's Pancake House and a Sign of Dr. Nash Memories	61
Chapter 30	An Evening Roaming the Cosmos	63
Chapter 31	The Tiny Door Behind the Curtain	65
Chapter 32	Miss Ida B.'s Evidence	66
Chapter 33	The Queen of Hearts	67
Chapter 34	And Then, I Rise	69
End Note	A Long Tale: Synchronicity and the Quantum Field	71
Afterword	Telescopes and Time Machines	75
Appendix A	"One Moment in Time"	77
Appendix B	Creative Writing as a Gesture in Synchronicity	79
Appendix C	Quantum Consciousness and Possibilities of Time Travel	83
Bibliography		87
Appendix D	Abstract. Time as Now. Here as Space: Neuroscience and Theory of Einstein Relativity	89
Appendix E	Abstract. Quantum Consciousness in the Extreme	91
About The Author		93

INTRODUCTION

This time, synchronicity began with butterflies in December of 2014. My father passed away in the beginning of the month and I searched for thank-you cards. Butterflies captured my attention on several stacks of cards, with extreme detail of embroidered black ink outlines and vivid colors of gold, red, and blue. I bought them and brought them home. I had also purchased Pam Grout's book $E=MC\,2$, because of my love of research and Einstein.

I sat for a few hours and wrote thank-you cards, noticing the butterflies on the cards as I wrote. I noticed the details of butterflies on my walls. They are real butterflies from South America framed by specialists of entomology in New York City.

When I took a break from writing, I began reading Pam Grout's book. I was surprised to see that she spoke about the observation of butterflies. Then the observation of pennies and how often the coins showed up in your life. I had already understood this process and collected butterflies throughout my house. I held one of the butterfly thank-you cards in my hands. A huge clear penny jug decorated my family room near the stone fireplace. Was it possible that one could visit the future and place sign posts as reminders of our journey and then return to the present? Was this another experience of how one can experience the notion of "quantum"? Physicists from

Princeton University talked about that possibility of time travel through courses on Einstein and relativity. It was at that moment I thought of the meaning of Jung's synchronicity and the possibility of time travel. Jung also wrote about events taking place at a future time and being represented in the present time as synchronicity or meaningful coincidence (Jung 1955:144-5).

When Einstein visited Zurich, Switzerland in 1909 and 1912, he often dined with Carl G. Jung, a Swiss psychologist and lecturer at Zurich University. Einstein's theories on relativity influenced the work of Jung. And so Jung writes, "It was Einstein who started me off thinking about a possible relativity of time as well as space. . . . More than thirty years later this stimulus led to my relation with the physicist Professor W. Pauli and to my thesis on synchronicity" (Jung 1976:109).

To Jung, space-time relativity was different. The conscious had similar qualities to quantum science. From Einstein's theory of relativity, Jung developed the definition of synchronicity as "conditioned relativity of space and time" (1952b, para. 840). He wrote about the timeless quality of the unconscious and space through quantum physics and also documented the influence of Albert Einstein in a letter:

> To Carl Seelig [Carl Seelig, the friend and first biographer (German-Swiss) of Albert Einstein]
>
> Dear Dr. Seelig, 25 February 1953
>
> I got to know Albert Einstein through one of his pupils, a Dr. Hopf, if I remember correctly.

Professor Einstein was my guest on several occasions at dinner, when, as you have heard, Adolf Keller was present on one of them and on others Professor Eugen Bleuler, a psychiatrist and my former chief.

These were very early days when Einstein was developing his first theory of relativity.

He tried to instill into us the elements of it, more or less successfully.

As non-mathematicians, we psychiatrists had difficulty in following his argument.

Even so, I understood enough to form a powerful impression of him.

It was above all the simplicity and directness of his genius as a thinker that impressed me mightily and exerted a lasting influence on my own intellectual work.

It was Einstein who first started me off thinking about a possible relativity of time as well as space. . . .

More than thirty years later this stimulus led to my relation with the physicist Professor W. Pauli and to my thesis of synchronicity.

With Einstein's departure from Zurich my relation with him ceased, and I hardly think he has any recollection of me.

One can scarcely imagine a greater contrast than that between the mathematical and the psychological mentality.

The one is extremely quantitative and the other just as extremely qualitative.

> With kind regards,
> Yours sincerely,
> C.G. Jung
> (Carl Jung, *Letters* Vol. II, pp. 108-9, https://carljungdepthpsychology.wordpress.com/2015/08/02/how-dr-jung-met-albert-einstein/)

As Professor J. Richard Gott of the Astrophysics Department at Princeton University has noted, "In the history of science, great breakthroughs often occur when someone realizes two situations thought to be different are actually the same or have a strong connection for further discovery."

And in my research and course study, synchronicity is the window, the key—this moment in time. Time travel into the future and back again to the present takes place in the quantum field and consciousness of mind.

FOREWORD
THE CONSCIOUS AS QUANTUM

It's a poor sort of memory that only works backwards . . .
Carl Jung's favorite quote about synchronicity from
<u>Through the Looking-Glass</u> by Lewis Carroll

How would the theories of Einstein and Jung play out in writing a novel about Princeton?

Let's go back to the beginning, with the writing of my first book called *Quantum Leaps in Princeton's Place*. I had interviewed the two oldest citizens in Princeton, New Jersey and placed the interviews away. There was no intention to write a book, but to document their lives living in Princeton for over one hundred years. The people I interviewed soon passed away, leaving their legacy and story in a documentary format. After six months had elapsed, my daughter Michaela had a play date with a new girl who was attending her school. As we drove through the mansions of Rosedale Road, we could not find the house as her new friend had described it to us.

Let's say that you are able to move into the future through time travel by means of your consciousness using quantum theory, Einstein's relativity, and synchronicity. Your future self who returns to your present knows that you are at the wrong door on Rosedale Road and that you have no intention of writing a book about the older people interviewed several months before. Your future self also knows that there is an important diary in the house that will connect the interviews you have conducted with the house and the story about Princeton that you will have the opportunity to tell.

You are knocking and because there is no answer and because you have knocked so long, you are about to turn away. For synchronicity to work, you need to be inside the Rosedale House to get the red diary. Your future self appears on the sidewalk walking perpendicular to the homes. As you view yourself leaving the Rosedale House, you see someone that looks like you who asks you if you are lost. Your present self admits you are a little lost and says the number of the house you are looking for. The person points out, "Why, it's just next door and that house does not have a number to identify it." You just missed it.

You say thank you to the person and head toward the house. Michaela comments how much the woman looked like an elderly version of you. You acknowledge but ignore her comment. You want to make sure this is the right house. You knock on the door. Then you wait for several minutes. Thinking there was no one at home again, we turn away and walk toward the car. But then, something happens. The door of the mansion slowly opens . . .

CHAPTER 1

A MAD HATTER'S TEA PARTY

"Wait!" a voice cried from behind the large white door. "Wait, you must be Michaela's mom." The door opened wide. A sudden gust of wind passed like a sigh. As the door opened, Michaela caught sight of her friend next to her mother. The home was beautiful and large. They had just moved in and I could see the boxes piled in the first parlor. The mansion was very old. She told me that it used to be a plantation house on many acres before it was later subdivided.

We sat down for tea while our children ran upstairs to play. "After tea, I want to give you a tour of the house," her mom said. "It's historical. It has four floors with the top floors which used to be slave quarters. Look what we found in this box in the basement."

She pulled out a dusty old box filled with old black and white photographs of the house. Then she handed me a red diary. "It belongs to Daisy, the owner of the mansion who wrote this in 1912. Amazing, isn't it?"

I looked at the diary with curiosity. I skimmed through a few pages and realized there was a connection between this and one of the people I interviewed several months before. Ms. Ida B. was here.

Within the diary, Ms. Ida B. was mentioned by name. I knew I had to write about this. The diary was the key to an important story that needed to be told.

I gasped. "Do you mind if I borrow this? You would not believe this, but an old woman I interviewed several months ago lived here. And her name is mentioned several times in this diary."

"Oh my, what a coincidence. I had no idea you wrote about people like this. And the coincidence of her name in this diary. I would have just left this in the basement when I found it and never mention it. It's a strange sort of find, you know. For some reason, I felt compelled to show it to you. Of course, you may borrow it. And every time Michaela comes over for a play date, feel free to write. You must write about this . . . ."

CHAPTER 2

DOWN THE RABBIT HOLE

As I looked back upon the circumstances and writing of my first novel, I wanted to understand more about synchronicity as a "moment" in time and consciousness as a possibility for time travel. Jung and Einstein had glimpses into this through their research. Princeton University, who maintains records of Einstein's research in relativity and active courses in quantum mechanics and astrophysics, was a great start for understanding the process. In addition, the research placed me at the heart of Princeton at the University and Princeton, the subject of my books. I was able to take these courses and see first-hand some of the important research in the field of quantum mechanics.

Professor Gott was one of the professors who wrote and taught one of the foundation courses. Students used his book and research as a main text in his course. His research explained time travel, quantum mechanics, and Einstein's theories of relativity. The books, *Cosmos, Quantum Mechanics, Quantum Physics, Time Travel in Einstein's Universe,* and *Foundations of Astrophysics,* expanded our knowledge of the planets, the universe, and black holes. These books helped us learn the important mathematical equations and problem solving that Einstein worked with in order to prove his theories about the quantum field and investigate the possibilities of time travel.

And this semester brought the NASA information and discovery of seven new Earth-like planets called the Trappist-1 series, orbiting a red dwarf star nearly forty light years away . . .

CHAPTER 3

GOLDEN AFTERNOONS AT PRINCETON UNIVERSITY

Princeton is a bustling but quiet town. It's difficult to find parking on the university campus. Of course, students and professors have parking permits cemented on their back windshields to park in prescribed lots. But these lots are far away from the destination of buildings and classrooms. If you want to get closer, you park next to a meter, feeding it quarters during a two-hour span. Or buy a "smart" card from the lot in the center of town that can hold sixty dollars-worth of meter time. Classroom lecture and library study time will quickly use the card up.

The afternoon sun was golden. It glowed and reflected golden slithers on the withered brown grass beneath my feet as I walked. It was my first day of classes at Princeton University. Crowds of students fill the streets and Gothic-style tunnels and pathways on campus. My courses in astrophysics were held in Peyton Hall in the afternoons. I searched for my building and classroom passing the oddly shaped library that stood next door.

My professor began her lecture. "The more we learn about the universe, the less we understand." Her words coincided with a tweet I saw on Twitter earlier the same day by Nassim Haramein, physicist and the Director of Research for the Resonance Science Foundation, who said, "The concepts of spirituality are typically the physics we haven't understood yet."

I knew I was in the right place.

I furiously took notes about the movement of planets, the discovery of dark energy, and the notion that we can see the past in what is our present through a single beam of light coming from a dead star at the other end of space many light years away. I wrote in my notes about the death of stars, their light as the remaining past shining back into the present . . .

CHAPTER 4

THE CHESHIRE CAT

One of the things I learned while taking coursework at Princeton University in astrophysics and quantum mechanics is that there is always talk about the real possibility of time travel based on scientific theories. This fourth dimension was discussed by Princeton scientist, J. Richard Gott in his book *Time Travel in Einstein's Universe*, used in the first course on astrophysics. There are four dimensions: length, height, depth, and time. Our consciousness moves along the time continuum from the beginning to the end of our lives.

Our universe is four-dimensional and represented in a quantum field. It's like the example I wrote about this experience in my journal regarding Jung's consciousness and synchronicity two years before taking my coursework at Princeton that verified my findings. In order to give you the exact location in the fourth dimension, you would need the location or corner you might find in New York City, 33 East Fifty-Second Street and 5th Avenue, 5th floor, and the exact time of 10:00 a.m. My moving into the future through a moment in synchronicity was like going to the tenth floor with information and returning to the fifth floor in the present moment of time.

Einstein used this idea in his theory of relativity in 1905. He laid the foundation of these paradoxes, knowing that our bodies and ideas could travel only as fast as the speed of light. And to support this, famous scientist Stephen Hawking noted that these light waves spread out like circular ripples in a pool creating a grand unified "theory of everything" or super string theory. These time dimensions can be dreamlike or experienced in a form of a consciousness moment, which could bring you into future time and back to the present, like Jung's ideas on synchronicity.

The discussions and research between Jung and Einstein from 1905 to 1912 laid the foundation for me to explore the idea of Jung's view of consciousness and Einstein's view and theory of relativity through the quantum field. If light can travel at its relative speed in the quantum field, then consciousness can travel at the speed of light from the present to the future and back again into the seemingly present "moment" of synchronicity, according to Einstein's theory of relativity which is now supported today by quantum physics.

In synchronicity, the moment of time of coincidence allows for possible time travel into the past and future back to the present. I soon discovered through my research that Jung's work specialized in the sub-atomic inner world of consciousness and thought, while Einstein's work dealt with the larger cosmos or universe. Both arenas mirror each other in the laws of physics. Together, their research would provide answers and possibilities about time. Time travel is made possible by observers who move relative to different views of time consciousness in the quantum field.

CHAPTER 5

IT'S ALL ABOUT TIME

One can hear the phantom sound of counting during dusk of day. "One, two, three . . ." the heavy breathless voice echoes and reverberates into silence near my classroom at Peyton Hall. It is Princeton University's crew team counting strokes on Carnegie Lake. Creeping across and slithering sideways against the wind in a practice. Timing in the sport of crew is everything.

Today on Saturday, I wait for my oil change at the local garage nearby. I see a display brochure sitting on a nearby window: *It's All About Time.* This serves as another moment of synchronicity for me as I realize through my research and daydream the connection between the quantum field and consciousness in time travel.

Not only was Einstein a great physicist, but he was a great believer of the power of the human mind. As Einstein said, "The intuitive mind is a sacred gift and the rational mind is a faithful servant. We have created a society that honors the servant and forgotten the gift." No wonder Jung and Einstein were close researchers at one time. Jung and Einstein were on their way to making an important discovery about the possibilities of time travel according to my research and readings. These readings, along with my research, allowed me to open the door to synchronicity and finally finish telling the story about Miss Ida B. from my first two novels, *Quantum Leaps in Princeton's Place* and *Six Doors Down*.

CHAPTER 6

HEAVEN IN A HOAGIE

There's a place down Nassau Street close to the university that opens at 10:00 in the morning until "LATE," so the front sign says. It is the small shop with an orange and black facade of university colors. It has large, cloudy panes of glass that diffuse upon the sidewalk at midday and glowing lights that penetrate the darkness outside at midnight.

Everyone at Princeton University knows of it because of the long lines at all times, especially in March during mid-term madness at midnight. High school students know of it because of the "Phat Lady" and "Heart Stopper" sandwiches piled with French fries and bacon atop a cheesesteak, drizzled with oil and vinegar. The place is called "Hoagie Haven."

Founded in 1976, the haven has fed thousands of sleepy-eyed and starving students.

Suddenly, I break out of my daydream by a deep booming voice as if from heaven saying, "Next!" I am now the person in line closest to the counter. My judgement day has come. I hesitate and then order the ham and cheese hoagie with oil and vinegar with a Coke.

As I squeeze through the crowded lines in the space to the door and leave, I chuckle and smile. For I'm just another hoagie junkie in Princeton headed to class with my fix for lunch today.

CHAPTER 7

BLACK SQUIRRELS AND TIGER TALES

The large, dusty, red brick buildings hover. Their pointed peaks signal the sky. The green-aged slate plates of roof hold folded, pale yellow, dim-lit, multi-paned windows that reflect the daylight. These are the famous frat mansions and eateries of Princeton University that house the elite. The looming buildings feed the streets with students during passing time. And across the street lies the sterile white Woodrow Wilson School, with its tall cement columns and long, thin, blurred eyes of cloudy glass.

There is a path, a shortcut, I use between this brick building with its golden number 13 nailed on the front door and the Cannon Club, with its huge ebony black cannon on the front lawn. It's like taking a walk through history to my science classes every time I go by.

The Cannon Club, the Eatery of the Ivy League, on my left as I walk, was founded in 1893 and occupied as a small house that the Tiger Inn used. On my right, thickets of dark green ivy decorate the grounds of the brick fraternity house with frolicking black squirrels. They dance and hang from the branches above. They squeeze and race around the buildings below.

Princeton seems to be the only place on the East Coast where one can find this breed of swinging black squirrel. They are friendly creatures, morphed from the same grey squirrel species. And there are many. According to myth, they emerged from the bowels of a biology basement filled of unauthorized experiments. These escapees now dominate the Princeton campus. Another myth tells us that a resident, Moses Taylor Pyne, imported black and orange squirrels to match the university's colors. But to this day, no orange squirrels have emerged.

Nevertheless, fearless black squirrels are a large part of the Princeton University experience. One can see them under the thick brush beneath thick oak trees, collecting food for winter. Their black bushy tails swish and twitch high in the air as they pretend to be the mascot for Princeton, wagging their imaginary tiger tails.

CHAPTER 8

PINK

Pink palettes of knit kitten hats with ears on every head bob like waves in a crowded sea. Then swell shades of rose-colored blush, fuschia, and flamingo. Ballet slipper pink, bubblegum, and strawberry crush. They swarm and squeeze into the National Mall in Washington, D.C. on January 21, 2017.

It is the greatest march for equality. It is energized and creative. It is peaceful and diverse. There are mothers and fathers. There are grandmothers, children, and babies. It is the Women's Day of Protest when millions take to the streets of major cities all over the world after the call on social media to knit thousands of pink hats to wear on that day in solidarity.

Luxury buses filled with women protesters left Princeton, New Jersey and headed to the nation's capital building. Chants echo the melody, "Women's rights are human rights!"

Princeton mayor Liz Lempert attended the protest in Trenton, New Jersey that started at the Trenton War Memorial and ended at the State House. "It is going to be more important than ever that people will stand up and be vocal about things important to them,"

Lempert said, "and to use our collective voice to make a strong statement."

"I'm so excited to be here and participate," Melinda Brown, a fifteen-year-old from Princeton attending the Washington, D.C. protest said. "I'm here with my mother to make history, but most of all to make a statement about women's rights and the future. We're not going away!"

CHAPTER 9
TAKING TO TWITTER

On Holocaust Remembrance Day, January 27, 2017, Twitter showed us photographs with the names of each Jewish person who came to the United States as refugees from their countries in Europe trying to escape from the Nazis. This exhibition was to show solidarity with Muslim people prohibited from entering the United States by means of a ban. One by one, we see the hope of life in their faces as they sought asylum in the United States by ship. But they were turned away by the United States and sent back where they later faced their deaths:

- 1939 Evelyn Greve: murdered in Italy.
- 1939 Ruth Karliner: murdered in Auschwitz.
- 1939 Erich Dublon: murdered in Auschwitz.
- 1939 Betty Kaufherr: murdered in Auschwitz.
- 1939 Maximillian Kohn: murdered in Auschwitz.

President Trump makes no mention of this day in any of his political comments. Last year, President Obama recognized the day in remembrance. "We are all Jews," he told the world.

CHAPTER 10

AIRPORTS, ATTORNEYS, AND OTHER EXPLANATIONS OF TIME TRAVEL

Some quantum physicists theorize that the universe contains many parallel world histories or possibilities. They liken the universe to a large train yard with switches to change the tracks in the procession of time. Accordingly, every time there is a group decision made or an electron of energy jumps randomly from one place in the universe to another, there is another possibility of our existence being experienced.

For example, we are on a train moving from the past to the present. We pass the events of World War I. Then we pass the events of World War II and the Korean War, then the Vietnam War. But now, in our present, can we suddenly change our current course with a group decision?

In our real-time scenario of February 2017, there is an executive order to send all Syrian refugees back to their countries where they face war and execution. The Syrian refugees are already in transit to the United States and become stranded in various airports throughout the world where they are denied entry.

A global group decision is made to protest this action and lawyers appear at airports to help all of the refugees gain entry into the United States. Federal judges stay up throughout the night to help file court papers to prevent the Syrian refugees from being sent away and gain safe passage into the United States. A temporary stop to the executive order is mandated and refugees are allowed to pass through. This group decision and action saves their lives and prevents future deaths, thus changing a historical course that the world never sees or experiences.

Quantum mechanics views the world with many of these parallels and possibilities. Something like a train railway can be switched by a decision before a major event, thus avoiding the event completely and creating another world history as we experienced in real time. In other words, individuals can join a collective consciousness and make the decision to do the right thing such as the global protest that protects refugees from going back to their countries where they face danger and execution. Other scientists explain time travel possibilities through the worm holes of the quantum fields, finding the shortcuts of history and science through space travel.

CHAPTER 11

THE POOL OF TEARS

Nowadays, one can take a tour of the campus and see Einstein's Lecture Hall at Princeton University. Einstein's tenure at Princeton University extended from 1933 through 1955. And today, I enter the room and listen to the echoes of my empty footsteps. I sit in silent soliloquy in the first row of 200 wooden scroll-like desks with chairs suspended on a single metal pedestal.

Luminescent light glows from each window pane in the long arched windows on one side of the wall. Light bounces and reflects along a line of lecture desks and the wooden floor because of the angle of the sun. It is as if the light knows it has always been the subject of conversation in this room and makes its energy deliberately known. The light travels across eight movable black chalk boards, screech-less and clean. Two large white scales hang high without weight at the very top of the front walls above the boards near the high ceiling in the lecture hall. Then a separate and lone professor's desk graces the scratched, worn wooden floor.

The lecture hall reminded me to revisit my interview notes from Miss Ida B. several years ago.

I took the notes from my bag and started to reread them. Again and again, I looked over the questions I had asked her about her mother's work at Princeton University. Through Miss Ida B.'s memory of her mother, Carnethia could see the university by doing evening work and cleaning in Einstein's Lecture Hall in the 1940s before women were admitted in 1969, way before people of color were accepted.

I imagined what it must have been like for women back then. . . . The thunder outside crackled suddenly and I could hear the rain slosh against the side of the wall where I sat beneath the vapor glow clouding the small panes of the window. Then it was as if the ceiling suddenly sprang a leak and water dripped and flowed like tears. It was from pain from the struggle: the woman's suffrage movements and the personal, female exclusions from society of all kinds.

It was like the water from the sweat that soaked Carnethia's clothing from unthankful and back-breaking day work cried. Tears from the sadness from the loss of a child leaving, now grown, choke and drown a mother in sorrow. It is the pain from splinters from washing wooden floor on hands and bended knee, while kneeling in prayer at the same time for forgiveness and salvation.

Tears of time passing, now dripping from the heavens fell cold onto my brown flesh. But creating puddles of my opportunity to grab hold of and step into, as I can now sit in the university classroom as part of the student body. Opportunities now pour and pursue my hands because of her. This was my sign post from the past, now visible in Einstein's room as the foundation of brown and black lives like the wooden floors, like the scrolled brown desks that she could never sit in to join the class in its quest for knowledge. It was her tears, Miss Ida B.'s mother, Carnethia, tumultuous tears that spackled the walls of segregation.

Her tears form pools of water beneath my feet. And I rise. I rise to get the janitor next door to clean the floor so no one falls. Rain water had poured from the ceiling leak onto the floor.

CHAPTER 12

LESSONS FROM A CATERPILLAR

A letter from a Princeton University administrator to W. E. B. Du Bois (quoted at the 10th anniversary conference of the Association of Black Princeton Alumni in 1977) said:

> We have never had any colored students here, though there is nothing in the University statutes to prevent their admission. It is possible, however, in our proximity to the South and the large number of Southern students here, that Negro students would find Princeton less comfortable than some other institutions.

It was not until World War II, when the federal government opened a Naval Training School at Princeton on October 5, 1942, that the color barrier was broken. Four Black students, John Leroy Howard, James Everett Ward, Arthur Jewell Wilson, Jr., and Melvin Murchison, Jr., entered the University through the United States Navy's V-12 program, with the first three earning undergraduate degrees. Howard was the first to receive a Princeton degree on February 5, 1947.

But colored people of that time could be hired to do housekeeping, cleaning, and gardening of the university grounds. Carnethia, Miss Ida B.'s mother, had just reduced her cleaning workload to weekends at the university because she was aging and having trouble getting around the large campus to complete larger assignments.

One night, as she was scrubbing the wooden floor of Einstein's lecture hall, she noticed a black fuzzy caterpillar creeping along the front of the lecture hall. She looked at it as if it were a nuisance and quickly attempted to pick it up. She huffed loudly.

"Leave it alone," a voice said. "It's not harming anyone. I actually like its quiet company."

She quickly turned around to see a man with gray feather-like hair at the opposite end of the lecture hall near the door.

"I don't understand why humans bother insects. They don't bother anyone," he continued.

Her eyes beamed upward as she froze. And she saw him for the first time. He had the familiar face that people talked about. Everyone knew him. His gray hair was wild and disheveled about his face. His grimace and wrinkles turned upward into a smile. He extended his hand toward her to help her from the floor.

"Miss, please don't take that posture. Please stand up," he said.

He was Albert Einstein.

"Sir, I was just finishin' up my cleanin' here. I'll be out of your way," Carnethia said as she started to move the mop and bucket through the door.

The Future is My Past

"Don't rush." Einstein said softly. "You have as long as you need."

Carnethia glanced up again. "You're that Einstein professor. The famous one."

"Some people say that. Some people don't even talk to me on campus. They think I am a little strange."

"But you're the famous professor . . ." Carnethia started.

"And what does that mean?" he asked her, rubbing his chin.

"I dunno. Famous. You know what famous means, I'm sure."

"Sometimes famous means lonely. Sometimes it means weird. And even sometimes it means that people discriminate against you. I guess you have felt that way too," Einstein said.

"Yes, yes. I have felt that way. Of course. All the time. But I'm not famous. I don't know what that's like. I can't even read. I hope my daughter will one day. She is away at college. At Tuskegee." Carnethia spoke as she stood hunched over, holding the mop top beneath her chin.

"I am sure you are proud," he said.

"And you can stand there and talk with me, huh?" Carnethia asked. "Most people don't see me cleanin' here. They don't hear me or see me. But you are talkin' with me. Isn't that strange for a famous professor, sir?"

"Of course, I can talk to you. And now, why not? Thank you for cleaning my lecture hall. A lot of students do not take care of it," Einstein said as he looked about the room. "And not everything looks as it seems. I do research here. I study. I teach. But there are people who discriminate against others. Even White people against White people. I know what it feels like to be laughed at. To be jeered at. But I know what and who is valuable in life."

Einstein comforted her. "Love the family you have. Your very special daughter. And tell her one day that you spoke to me. She probably won't believe it."

"Yes, sir," Carnethia chuckled.

It had been a long time that she had laughed with someone so heartily as he closed the door.

CHAPTER 13

THE HEART-SHAPED PIN

Last night, I remembered that Miss Ida B. had told me about a special heart-shaped pin that her mother received that caused her mom, Carnethia, to change her way of thinking about her life. I realized this was perhaps a jinn of sorts that needed to be mentioned in my third book because now it made sense with the science courses I was taking at Princeton University. The idea of a jinn comes from Russian theoretical astrophysicist Igor Novikov, who wrote *Black Holes and the Universe* (1995). In time travel, a jinn is an object that behaves like a particle in quantum physics. The particle can suddenly appear through a shortcut in space like the other side of a wormhole or space tunnel. And there are many ways of playing out an event in a parallel universe of consciousness.

I had forgotten about this and never wrote the thoughts down in my notes, but had the idea from the interviews. Oblivious, I went to the Barnes and Noble bookstore the next day to purchase Godiva chocolates since the day before was Valentine's Day and one can get chocolates for half price. Then the cashier started talking to me. She was an older woman with gray hair and a crooked smile.

As she rang up my order, she told me that she was an artist and made heart pins for people. Her pins are special and she makes them out of love. She explained that kindness begets another kindness. She even hates to charge people for pins she makes. I suddenly realize a connection of synchronicity. I glanced at her as if she knew that was something I needed to remember: to put the heart-shaped pin in my third novel from last night—and she knew nothing about me or the novel I was writing. Another moment of synchronicity! So I immediately sat down and wrote so I would not forget—I suddenly found myself back at the university.

As I saw Miss Ida B.'s mom, Carnethia, crying, I stood by the doorway of Einstein's lecture hall and watched. I wanted to do something. I wanted to save her, but knew that the history of this country stood in my way. I did have something to give to her. It was a kind word, a pat on the shoulder, and a heart-shaped pin I always wore on my lapel.

As I quietly walked toward her, she looked up. Her eyes were bloodshot and she sniffled a few times as she looked up at me. "Child, you are not supposed to be in here . . ."

"I know. I'm sorry. I'm sorry to see you cry. I have something to give you. I know I don't really know you." I stretched out my hand and took the heart-shaped pin from my lapel. "This is for you. It is mine. It reminds me to always give the gift of love. Love is free. And when I wear it, I feel special. I always feel like a queen . . ."

"Queen? Huh." she shrugged. "I'm just tired. Overly tired of everythin'. Just lost my daughter to college at Tuskegee. She's gone off without permission. She was everythin' I got. Everythin' I've worked for. I have nothin' left."

"I'm sure she will come back to you." I tried to comfort her.

"I shouldn't take this from you. It must be precious to you." Carnethia whimpered as she shook her head from side to side.

"Please. I saw you crying. I want you to feel better. Please take it for yourself and know you are loved," I said as I placed the pin in her wrinkled, wet hands. "I must go now. I should not be here. I will let myself out downstairs. I know the way," I said as I closed the door and disappeared into the tranquil sunlight at dusk.

I saw the walls in the lecture hall grow dark around her. Carnethia remained in the deep, dreary shadows of the building. I was leaving her too, like her daughter, with the chill of desertion. She watched me helplessly. I scurried away from the lecture hall down the slate stairs and out the front door.

CHAPTER 14

BLESS "SAID" BE THE PEACE MAKERS

Somehow I feel swept up by a whirlwind and tossed about in February of 2017. I'm not in America anymore. And I'm certainly not in Oz. Maybe the dystopian novel *1984*? Or worse yet, the 1930s?

During the 1930s, the Anti-Defamation League fought the KKK. Hitler came to power in Europe. The NAACP engaged in peaceful protests and fought legal challenges of discrimination in the courts.

But today, in 2017, we have taken a similar journey back into time. There have been about 700 hate incidents reported since the Presidential election, according to the Southern Poverty Law Center in Montgomery, Alabama.

I am reminded of my McCloy Fellowship in Journalism in Germany that I was awarded and researched. The work is archived in the Holocaust Museum in Washington, D.C. I interviewed and photographed some of the oldest Holocaust survivors in 2000. We walked through the Dachau camp. We cried. We thought that this can never happen again. That was the reason for documenting the events. But now, I quickly remember that the words of hate came first. Then the propaganda. And then the bystanders who said nothing.

Now, at this time of giving and gratitude, love and thanks . . . this needs to be said. It needs to be pointed out. For America, this is all very real for us now.

Congressman John Lewis, who lived a life of peaceful protest for Civil Rights, says, "Accept a way of peace, believe in the way of love, believe in the philosophy and discipline of nonviolence. Never become bitter. Never become angry." And we are reminded by the Anti-Defamation League during its Summit on Anti-Semitism on November 16, 2016, in New York City that "Never is Now."

Now, test the truth in the news for yourself and do not believe in untruth and propaganda. Our personal freedoms are closely linked to freedom of the press. Freedom of press organizations help preserve our basic rights of speech.

Last, we must remember and not be deceived: A divided America is not a strong America . . .

This morning, I bought a cup of coffee before entering my train. I handed the cashier a dollar bill that we all use in America all the time, every day, that says "In God We Trust."

At first, I thought, "Heaven, help us." But then later looked up the significance of the motto in our country's history. The phrase first appeared in 1864 with religious intent by a Pennsylvania minister. But ironically it had a more significant meaning during the Cold War. The phrase was printed on all American currency in 1955 as a cold cultural war against Communism that did not believe in a god.

Are you shivering yet?

CHAPTER 15

TWEETS AND LEAKS, FAKE NEWS, OH, MY!

It looked like a schizophrenic episode in a vision of Dr. John Nash in film on the Princeton University campus. Spies trampling the grounds with flashlights at midnight and asking him for special codes. But newly appointed Flynn had really spoken to the Russians and lied about his encounter with the Russians. He was immediately fired by newly elected Donald Trump which launched a national investigation about the recent Presidential campaign of 2016.

In a strange juxtaposition of events, my husband and I decided to watch a movie we had missed in the theaters that same evening called *Bridge of Spies*, starring Tom Hanks. The film is set in 1957 at the height of the Cold War between the United States and the Soviet Union. At that time, both sides feared annihilation due to nuclear capabilities. A suspected Russian spy named Rudolph Abel is picked up, tried, and convicted in court.

The climax of the movie brings us to the Glienicke Bridge in Germany for an exchange of spies. It is dark and quiet. The figures stand in silent silhouette amid the towers filled with trained sharpshooters. The tension drags on a bit and nothing is happening on screen. I pick up my phone and quickly look at my Twitter feed.

I see a March 2017 article tweeted by *The Washington Post* called "Everything You Need to Know about Trump and Russia." It says that the Trump team ties to Russia are "fake news," yet those who leaked the information for those articles needed to be found and punished.

President Trump got to know Russian President Vladimir Putin "very well," but he doesn't know Putin. And Jeff Sessions "did not have any communications with the Russians," except for the two meetings with Sergey Kislyak he forgot to mention under oath for the position of Attorney General. So Sessions recuses himself from any investigation. But Trump says there is no reason for Sessions to recuse himself.

The music intensifies. The tension mounts on the television screen. I look up. I gasp as I await the shots that are never fired. The two spies are finally exchanged from each side of the bridge. Tom Hanks is relieved. The screen darkens. The scene ends.

But stay tuned. It's not over yet. "I Spy" another Russian and Trump episode within the next few weeks.

CHAPTER 16

PRINCETON: A SANCTUARY CITY

Some children are afraid of the dark. They are afraid someone will snatch them away from their families. Their mamas and papas try to console them. But they do not sleep. Nowadays, their fears are real. These are the children of the undocumented. Immigrants who came to America searching for a dream.

I used to teach English as a Second Language many years ago in Princeton Schools K-12 at Riverside Elementary School and Princeton High School. Our district had more than thirty-six different languages and dialects then: Spanish, Italian, Creole, French, Arabic, and Quechua, to name a few. We used to visit each other in our homes and have meals together. We used to dance and sing songs in their languages. And I still know some of their families all of these years. They are life-long friends. Some are well documented with visas and green cards, but others are undocumented, mainly from Guatemala.

Now, they remain hidden. It is as if shadows engulfed and stifled their breath. They are afraid to play in the streets. They are afraid to tell people their names. Children are fearful they will lose their parents.

After the Trump immigration deportation orders of February 2017, Princeton officials countered the effects upon immigrants in the town. The town, a sanctuary city, has had information sessions for immigrants to educate them on what to do if they encounter immigration authorities and how to prepare in the event they are separated from their children.

"I am very happy Princeton is a sanctuary city," a friend of a Honduran family told me. "We know the authorities here care about us and will do everything to help us out."

Another mother said, "We are lucky here in Princeton, but this order comes from President Trump and we still are not sure everything will be okay for us."

Even Elisa Neira, the municipal human services director, agrees, "So it's really difficult times to really provide concrete information or reassure people that nothing bad is going to happen."

And there is real room for worry. The Department of Homeland Security under President Trump intends to hire 10,000 more agents in order to implement the deportation orders signed in his executive order. "All of those in violation of immigration law may be subject to immigration arrest, detention, and, if found removable by final order, removal from the United States."

Local police in Princeton will not enforce immigration law as the Trump administration encourages. A sanctuary city seeks to protect all of its citizens within its jurisdiction. This includes undocumented immigrants living in Princeton.

Mayor Liz Lempert adds, "This interferes with all of the work they've been doing to build stronger relationships with the community."

But there is still fear lurking in the street shadows.

"This is a nightmare," an undocumented father tells me. "I pray that I will wake up and this nightmare will go away and we are safe again."

CHAPTER 17

THIS IS NOT AMERICA

It is an unusual friendship: Michael and Hilde, Gunnar and Jack. They have over seventy years of age difference, but one can see them together each day smiling and laughing.

Like Michael and Gunnar, Viola, an eighteen-year-old with brown glowing eyes and long, flowing curly hair, also participates in the same program and helps Holocaust survivors, "My grandmother was a member of the S.S. Guard during Hitler's time, "Viola said. "She used to tell me stories of capturing Jews in the woods nearby our house. I am glad I can at least change history now and make life better. I show people the next generation can change the world."

I met these young people and the Holocaust survivors they helped in Berlin, Germany in the year 2000. I received funding through the McCloy Fellowship from the American Council on Germany and Harvard University to cover children and the Holocaust in Germany. While we were there, we were also able to document the lives of these young people through photographs and interviews. They legally traded their military service for helping Holocaust survivors over the age of eighty-five live their day-to-day lives.

Michael reads from the Hebrew Scriptures since Hilde's eyes have aged. Gunnar buys and brings daily groceries to Jack. "I feel I am doing a good service. People like Jack have suffered a lot and deserve to have a better existence for the rest of his life."

The work from this documentary project was later accepted into the archives of the Holocaust Museum in Washington, D.C. It was a work of remembrance: never to let the Holocaust happen to people again. But I have learned that memories, unless revived and kept in the forefront of our lives, can be short-lived.

An orange swastika appears spray-painted on a steel sculpture on the Princeton University campus the next morning between the Lewis Library and Peyton Hall, the building where I attend my astrophysics classes. The swastika is looming and large, a reflection of what is happening since the Trump election of 2016.

Tombstones lay toppled and desecrated across America. There has been a 94% increase in attacks on cemeteries and Jewish organizations since the beginning of the year of 2017, according to the Southern Poverty Law Center. And the Jewish Community Center Association of North America reported that twenty-one Jewish institutions, including day schools with children, received bomb threats during the first week of March.

But nowadays, people are standing together. Donations from thousands of Muslims and others pledged financial support of the Jewish organizations with more than $136,000 to help and repair damages.

David E. Posner, the Jewish Community Center's director of strategic performance, said in a statement, "Actions speak louder than words. Members of our community must see swift and concerted action from federal officials to identify and capture the perpetrator or perpetrators who are trying to instill anxiety and fear in our communities."

Hate still hurts. It even kills as it did in the Holocaust. We must remember for a reason and support others, no matter their race or religion. And never say that it cannot happen here.

CHAPTER 18

THE CASE OF WOODROW WILSON REVISITED

Old names on structural buildings, representing a segregationist past, are hard to erase. But on March 2017, the Woodrow Wilson School of Public and International Affairs at Princeton University sought to establish a historical marker that "educates the campus community and others about the positive and negative dimensions of the controversial Wilson legacy." This historical marker could be a monument, memorial, work of art or a digital exhibit.

Woodrow Wilson served as the thirteenth president of the University and the twenty-eighth president of the United States.

Cecilia Rouse, dean of the Woodrow Wilson School, said, "Our goal is to create an honest, thought-provoking marker that will convey the complexities of Wilson's legacy. This marker will not only draw attention to the person but also contribute to the overall identity of the Woodrow Wilson School."

In a letter in the *Princeton Alumni Weekly Magazine* of March 2017, alumnus Jeffrey B. Perry, Class of 1968, suggested the marker represent Hubert H. Harrison, the founder of the New Negro Movement of the early 1900s. Harrison worked against the backdrop of Wilson's America, with its rampant racism, segregation, and lynching.

Harrison's protest work and writings for the New Negro Movement was a request for respectability in a democracy. He fought against the slave narratives and demanded recognition for the education, refinement, and money that New Negroes had acquired for a place in society as equals.

But structural racism remains in place as a historical marker for America. It is a marker in our housing, our policing, our employment discrimination, and anti-Black, anti-Muslim, anti-Semitic hate crimes. Learning the truth of the past and educating future generations will begin the process of change. But real change demands truth, persistence, and love with the power to chisel through the walls of hatred in hearts.

CHAPTER 19

LIGHTS, CAMERA, ACTION!

The building looks like something out of the 1950s. It is small, beige with green trim. It has an entrance with a peaked green-trimmed roof. And in the center, a small rotunda-shaped space for a teller. A white marquee announces the selection of movies for the day: *Fences, I Am Not Your Negro,* and *The Salesman.* It is the Princeton Garden Theater on Nassau Street.

Built in the 1920s, the theater has always been a centerpiece for the Princeton community and culture. Although small in appearance, the theater seats 180 moviegoers and possesses the upgraded amenities of high-definition sight and sound on two screens.

The theater shows classic and foreign film and Oscar-winning shows. There are lively art shows and special events of interest to the community, including *The National Theater Live: Amadeus.*

It is a magical place where kids are not forgotten with the showing of *The Muppets Take Manhattan.*

Before each showing, the theater plays a special PSA by its own Oscar-nominated actor Ethan Hawke, who attended the Princeton Hun School nearby in 1988.

It is an extra special gathering place this year. The theater was nominated and voted to be "Best Movie Theater in New Jersey" by nj.com for 2017. And the popcorn was voted as a plus of all the finalists nominated for this honor.

Through community membership, gifts, and admission fees, the theater continues to be well funded and brings in all people within the college and community.

Coming to this theater near you in Princeton is the film *Deconstruction of the Beatles' Sgt. Pepper*. "It's a day in the life and I read the news today, oh boy . . ."

CHAPTER 20

THERE'S NO PLACE LIKE HOME

Eight-year-old Christina loves to move her body. When African drums play, it is her cue to get up and dance. Christina attends Johnson Park School in Princeton. She is American, but has spent most of her life living abroad in Africa.

"African weddings are quite beautiful," said Christina, with wide hazel eyes that luminesce like high-beam headlights and blonde pigtails.

Christina lived eight years in Tanzania, south of Kenya and north of Mozambique. Christina's family lived on the coast where temperatures were hot and humid, about 90 degrees. "I miss the beach the most," Christina said. "I never missed a day swimming in it!"

Tamara Martin, Christina's mother and missionary with Africa's Evangelical Organization, misses the beach also. She enjoyed building a conference center and helping the local church learn about the Bible. "It's challenging adjusting to life again in the United States," she said.

The biggest adjustment for her two children in school is language. In Tanzania, school is taught in Swahili, with English as the second language. But Christina and her brother, Kyle, were home-schooled by their mother in Africa. Home-schooling provided both children with flexible schedules for reading and writing.

But the larger class sizes in Princeton are foreign to Christina and Kyle. Although Christina loves writing and storytelling, she dislikes reading and television. She does not know all the sight words for reading in English on her grade level. "Reading is hard in English," said Christina.

Her classroom teacher reads with Christina every day, but this is the subject she absolutely loathes. "I don't think I like English," she said. "Swahili is so much easier for me."

When asked about her favorite subject, Christina responded, "Animals. I love animals and science. In Tanzania, we get to play with the wild life. We all live in a big zoo." She smiled.

The family longs to return to their small home in Africa at the end of the school year. They say that life in America can be too hectic. "The children come home every day exhausted from school. It is a technology overload they are not used to," their mother commented.

For now, Christina plays with her two black labs and Siamese cat. She pretends they are zebras and lions hiding in the brush and twisted thorn bushes of her backyard. Sometimes Christina thinks she can still hear the beach. Christina smiles and then sighs. She looks forward to going back to Africa, her home.

CHAPTER 21

SACRED SECRETS

African American children play in the wood. One peeks around the bark trunk of a huge tree and hugs it with a smile. Another stands still in the shadow of branches, covering her mouth with tiny hands to stifle a laugh. They are hidden, frozen in time as a secret sculpture garden. Their stone statues cry out history in a future memorial museum proposed for 2018 in the Sourland Mountains.

The Sourland Mountain Preserve lies on the northwestern border of Princeton. It is 4,000 acres of pines and maples that lie undisturbed by civilization. It is known for its nesting birds and decorative fall foliage. And hidden within the woods of the region is a burial ground of historical merit for African Americans and veterans dated from 1858.

The burial area is home to a one-room white-peaked building, the African Methodist Episcopal Church, on Hollow Road. Built in 1850, this historical find is now destined to be the first African American Museum in Central Jersey to be opened next year.

A variety of sculpture depicting the African American experience in New Jersey will be built and artifacts acquired for the property.

The concept is inspired by the sculptural design of the Whitney Plantation Museum in Louisiana.

It is the hope that future visitors will understand what the people who lived here experienced in their lives. Their lives will no longer be a secret hidden by the quietness of the woods and the coldness of the ground.

CHAPTER 22

A MATHEMATICAL CONSTANT

It is Pi Day in Princeton, the mathematical constant of 3.14 that corresponds directly to Albert Einstein's date of birth of March 14. It is a coincidence connected to his genius, some say. Maybe, but certainly a modern major event in Princeton that is all things Einstein.

Ride the train called "The Dinky" that leaves from Princeton Junction as it chugs into downtown Princeton and ride with Albert Einstein impersonators. Meet other impersonators of Einstein at his town home and learn more about him there.

Take the Pi bike tour at the Kopp Cycle Shop on 38 Spring Street and bike on the same roads that Einstein traveled on. The bike tour is 9.86 miles round trip (exactly 3.14 x 3.14) and the tour price is $31.41.

At the Morven Museum on Stockton Street, visitors wait in the dark to surprise an Einstein impersonator. All the children there think Einstein is lost again and may not show up. But he does not disappoint and shows up when the lights come on.

Einstein said, "Mozart's music is so pure and beautiful that I see it as a reflection of the inner beauty of the universe." So in tribute to Einstein at Richard's Auditorium on the Princeton University campus, there are concerts of Mozart's sonatas.

There is even a Pizza Pi contest and an Albert Einstein look-alike contest for children and older adults.

While researching and writing about this Pi Day, I grab a cup of coffee and look at the time on the clock. It is exactly 3:14 on 3/14. It is Pi-squared, another synchronicity! And a reminder from the Universe that in Princeton today, everything is quantum. And the quantum field is divine!

CHAPTER 23

WHO STOLE THE ART OF NEWS?

In an era when journalist organizations are banned from White House Press briefings and new words like fake news, alternative facts, and post-truth erupt each day, one may wonder about the state of new journalism in a post-Obama world. News journalism is certainly an art when it is reported accurately with the verifiable truth. But journalists worry that in the cosmos of social media, Facebook may be the only source of news people rely upon.

Facebook, the social media leader, uses advertisements, but controls the type of news one receives by the simple click of like, comment, or share. These choices are made by algorithms that monitor users' interests and then "feed" them what they believe the users wish to read while filtering out material users are supposed not to want.

The *Washington Post* reports that Facebook has been noted to report inaccurate trends in news through its non-human editors. Therefore, readers do not always have the alternate views of true news journalism. One reads news that Facebook thinks one wants to hear. This phenomenon is dangerous to readers of the news and news journalists who report the news, resulting in the loss of jobs to the rising giant and delivery of a product of the news that is not completely accurate.

Today, the Pew Center of Research reports that millennials (those born between 1981 and 1996) get 61% of their news from Facebook.

But in a survey of sixty young people between the ages of 14 and 17 in the Princeton area and personal discussion with ten of them, we learn something different and refreshing.

None of these younger teenagers use Facebook as a news source. All said they looked at *CNN, The New York Times,* and *The Wall Street Journal* as reliable news sources. And all said they learned how to research and validate their news sources in history, science, and language arts classes. "Facebook is only for my friends," Sara, a seventeen-year-old, said.

Anna, a sixteen-year-old junior, commented, "Usually with printed material that is fact-checked, written, and supplemented by experts, there is very little to be concerned about other than the author's credibility and bias."

"I believe it is essential to gather information from primary and secondary reliable sources so that viewers can trust the new source," Rupa, a fifteen-year old, commented. "This is important because inaccurate presentation of important events can lead to misunderstandings. I always double-check my news sources when I read news."

Bianca, a fourteen-year-old freshman, summed it up: "Current events is history in the making and good writing is an art, but truth in news is crucial to our press freedom."

CHAPTER 24

THE FREEDOM TO WRITE: A JOURNALIST'S STORY

Journalists in the metropolitan area of New York and throughout the country were surprised to receive a letter from our counterparts outside of our borders. But this story affects our livelihood and our Constitutional Rights of freedom in the United States. Anyone who likes to write and read should read this letter missed by the masses during the first several months of 2017:

> MEXICAN JOURNALISTS TO U.S. COLLEAGUES: 'WE NEVER BELIEVED THIS DAY WOULD COME'
>
> To our colleagues in the United States of America,
>
> At this time of an unprecedented, relentless assault on the free press of the United States by the Trump administration, we Mexican journalists, writers, and publishers stand in solidarity with you as you do your crucial work.

For decades you have stood by us as successive governments and criminal gangs have targeted our press and assassinated our journalists for doing work in the public interest—uncovering crimes and corruption. And so many times we have only known the truth about our own country by reading the stories followed and uncovered in the U.S. press. We urge you to continue to uphold freedom of expression as your society, institutions, and values depend upon it.

You have stood with us during the darkest hours of press freedom in Mexico and, although we never could believe this day would come, we now stand with you.

>Most sincerely,
>Jennifer Clement
>President, PEN International
>President Emeritus PEN Mexico
>Homero Aridjis
>President Emeritus, PEN International
>Lucinda Kathmann
>Vice President, PEN International
>President Emeritus, PEN San Miguel

And over 300 individual signatures by Mexican journalists.

(This letter originally appeared on the website of PEN International. https://pen.org/mexican-journalists-stand-solidarity-us-journalists/)

CHAPTER 25

THE CHARTER SCHOOL QUADRILLE

Public schools and charter schools continue their dance for dominance. One step forward, two steps back. And the confirmation of the new U.S. Secretary of Education, Betsy DeVos, under the Trump administration has intensified the music.

The Princeton Charter School was just approved to expand its ranks within the next two years to include 76 more students by a decision made by Acting New Jersey Education Commissioner, Kimberley Harrington. The provision allows students to be accepted by means of a lottery system.

The current charter school has an enrollment of 348 students. But this new provision allows for 1.16 million dollars more to be taken from the local tax dollar base. Five million dollars is already taken to maintain the current charter budget.

The decision is opposed by Princeton Public School Superintendent Stephen C. Cochrane and the Princeton Board of Education. "This is deeply disappointing," Cochrane said.

And the disappointment will show itself through teacher lay-offs and decreased programming for the public schools. Other nearby districts are also feeling the pain of charter schools. In nearby

East Brunswick, the charter school is not held accountable for its finances and how it spends tax dollars. It is difficult to locate the school's budgets and monitor its spending, but public schools must publish their budgets. Public schools hold to a different standard of transparency.

Some wonder if this is just the beginning of the deconstruction of the public school system and unions. Others, like the newly appointed DeVos, believe there is liberation for education with school choice through the voucher and charter school system.

In the meantime, Princeton Public Schools have decided to appeal the current decision with hopes of maintaining a diverse and public community school district with the utmost highest standards.

CHAPTER 26

THE SNOW QUEEN'S BALLET GROUNDS

Upstairs and next door to MCaffrey's Grocery Store, one finds the Princeton Ballet School, home of the American Repertoire Ballet Company since 1954. Within its walls, one hears classical music played live on piano for the dancers, young and old, as they "pas de bouree" across the floors.

At first, the musical combination throughout the halls sounds like a dueling duet of discord for dominance. But if you listen closely to the beats between the music, one can hear a rhythm. A distinctive rhythm that moves the body beyond ballet, jazz, and modern dance and coming from one particular room.

It's Hammer Time! Break-It-Down for a Hip Hop class on the ballet grounds. Angela Cusumano, choreographer and instructor, has been teaching this style of dance here since 2008. The class is a fusion of funky street jazz and bold creative choreography. With a warm-up of stretching and strengthening of the body, she moves her dancers through a technique of hip-hop walks and combinations across the floor. Her dance technique is hard-hitting with striking precision to beats and rhythms from Beyoncé to Bruno Mars.

People of all ages enjoy the dance style of Hip Hop and Angela's full and energetic classes demonstrate this fact. The dance form has crossed all religions, races, and cultures. Hip Hop has demolished stereotypes for Muslims and even remixed certain styles of classical ballet.

The dance history of Hip Hop moves date back to the late 1960s with pop, locks, and spins. And it has eventually evolved into a hot, global spectacular of competitions, performances, and You-Tube videos.

Nowadays, even the Snow Queen of Ballet melts to the heat and the beat of this cross-cultural craze and choreography. And Angela's classes in Princeton know how to break it all down.

CHAPTER 27

STEALING TIME

Before my science classes at Princeton University, I sit on Prospect Street. Waiting in my car. Watching time. Watching the meter tick down before my next lecture. Then I can put enough quarters in its mouth to cover the time on the meter that I will use in class.

People will tell you that finding a meter in Princeton can be challenging. There is only a two-hour limit on Prospect Street where the meters are closest to the classrooms.

Here, one can see the coins slip through slots like mouths methodically opening on their silver metal meter faces. They gulp until they are full with two hours and then slowly chip away the minutes. Some classes are three hours long and require students to disappear during the middle of class to nurture and feed. My classes are only an hour and twenty minutes, precisely within the time limit of walking to class and back. Then an extra five minutes added on just in case the professors go over their time limits for their lectures. It is the daily decorum nowadays for being respectful and polite.

At precisely the second, meter maids monitor the silver beasts. Taming them and relieving them of their metal meals. The maids stop and write furiously next to the cars that do not follow the rules, and with a quick snap, paste a white ticket on windshields. They shame the drivers who have looked away from their watches and clocks of minutes, the seconds, their time.

And car drivers looking for a parking space, beware: A parking ticket in Princeton is $40.00. And if you collect two tickets on your record without payment, you can actually be arrested. Then taken from the university streets in bright silver handcuffs by the police like a suspected criminal as the meter sparkles in the sunlight and joyously jeers behind you.

So, to prevent such exposure, I sit and wait in my car next to the silver meter. My watch and the meter ticking simultaneously, with the inner beating of my life's own heart rhythm waiting, just stealing time.

CHAPTER 28

THEORIES OF RACIAL RELATIVITY HIDDEN IN A HOUSE

Deep in the dark Herrontown Woods near the Princeton-Kingston line lies abandoned knowledge about Princeton University boarded up in the silence of a cottage. Decayed tree branches block the path to the house dilapidated with mold and age. Earth time has sealed its story. But preservationists have uncovered its scientific connection. They bring a discovery to light in the field of mathematics and physics.

It is not a special spatial equation. It is not a hidden telescope spanning the stars. But it is a story seeking racial equality, led by Princeton mathematics professor Oswald Veblen, whose work contributed to atomic physics and the theory of relativity. It is his cottage that lies decayed, a dormant secret in the woods today.

Dr. Veblen taught at Princeton University from 1905 to 1932 and later founded the Institute for Advanced Study. Not only did he offer a faculty appointment to Albert Einstein back then, but he was the first professor to fight for the admission of "coloured" faculty to Princeton University. He presented African American professor

William Waldron Shieffelin Claytor, a PhD. in mathematics from West Virginia State University, to the hiring board, but Princeton University denied his appointment due to race.

Four years later, Veblen was able to make another offer for employment to Dr. Claytor because the Institute for Advanced Study, where he now worked, had no discriminatory policies. Disillusioned by the passage of time, Claytor refused. But interestingly, in his old appointment, he would later become the professor who taught Katherine G. Johnson. She was the African American engineer who later worked for NASA, verifying the trajectory orbit for astronaut John Glenn, and featured in the movie *Hidden Figures*.

When Veblen died in 1960, his house in the woods remained dormant. And today, the house still continues to be swallowed up by green grassy overgrowth and dead spiraling vines spinning their own web within the boarded disarray. Red spray-painted graffiti on the house screams the message, "This was my house."

Although his house is on the list for rescue and preservation as a meeting house for scholars, money must be raised for repairs and restoration. His house holds histories of positive racial relativity and scientific achievements in math and physics. Its secrets deserve to be told and its knowledge made known as this notable math figure attempted to break barriers of race.

CHAPTER 29

PJ'S PANCAKE HOUSE AND A SIGN OF DR. NASH MEMORIES

The next day was a rainy May afternoon and on my way to study at the Princeton Library, I stopped in for pancakes at PJ's in Princeton Junction. The original pancake house is in Princeton on Nassau Street and is legendary since 1962, known for its starving student menu of waffles, pancakes, and eggs of any style. The lines of people parade in overflow through the door outside into the street.

As I was eating my favorite banana and whipped crème pancakes, I looked up and was surprised by a sign on the wall above my booth. I had eaten here many times, but never noticed the sign until this day. Maybe because I was sitting in a different booth than usual that housed the one and only 8x12 brown-framed sign on the wall. The sign read:

In honor of a great man with a beautiful mind,
this table is dedicated in Memoriam to
JOHN NASH
Where he often sat to eat
Here at PJ's Pancake House

Dr. Donna Clovis

I was sitting in his seat, in his booth. A feeling of warmth came over me and I took a moment to remember the kindness of the man, his wife, and his son who used to live just live six doors down from us in the Berrien section of Princeton Junction.

CHAPTER 30

AN EVENING ROAMING THE COSMOS

At Princeton Public Library Author's Day for my book signing of *Six Doors Down,* my friend Giordana came and brought a few additional friends. Her friend, Maureen, knew of another hidden gem of local lore about the town of Princeton. It was about an actress who later played the role of the Cat Woman in the *Batman* TV series and film during the late 1960s. After the book signing, I interviewed her and did some research . . .

A sultry singer and scientist rendezvous at the house of Einstein in Princeton this evening.

Miss Eartha Kitt, the famous singer and actress, always wanted to meet the genius physicist. Then through a series of letter requests from a friend who knew Einstein's secretary, Kitt was able to set up a date in January of 1955.

The tall, thin African American woman knocked on his door and entered. She had a chic style of elegance. She transfixed audiences with her mesmerizing voice on Broadway, national tours, and film. Kitt could sing in ten different languages and had performed on the stages of more than one hundred countries.

The stars were bright that evening and twinkled a special

ambiance of conversation. It was an evening to be remembered. For she was a star on the Hollywood Walk of fame and he was the twilight in the cosmos of time.

What does genius speak about on a date? Their conversation ranged from the origins of the Earth to the evolution of theater traditions. Einstein never watched and did not have a TV.

News of their meeting got out to the media and was published in several newspapers throughout the country. And this is how Maureen heard about the story back then.

CHAPTER 31

THE TINY DOOR BEHIND THE CURTAIN

A crowd emerges from the darkness of the brick archway into the glowing sunlight. It is a tour group of the incoming freshmen accepted by the university who look out onto Prospect Street and Washington Road. Their eyes are large, looming across the street with the excitement of possibilities. A few venture downwards on the stairs. Others take a careful gaze from the top landing, like a precipice above rugged ledge cliffs.

And the large sycamore trees whisper "Carpe Diem, Seize the day . . ." As if they remember the utterance of those words by the Roman poet Horace more than 2,000 years ago. The eventuality of mankind always being the same, four years will merge quickly into memories, measurements of years, days, and seconds of time. And the process of the young will change into the old and turn into a history.

Nowadays, time tweeted on their phones as hashtag #EinsteinIWTYE

"Imagination will take you everywhere."

CHAPTER 32

MISS IDA B.'S EVIDENCE

As I read through my interview notes about Miss Ida B. again, I realized that her mom gave her a special homecoming gift from college when Ida visited her mother at the Rosedale House. It was a heart-shaped pin. Carnethia told Ida she had missed her so much and realized that she needed to be kinder, even though they lived in the difficult times of segregation. Carnethia told her that the pin reflected her mother-daughter love and, like the rainbow promise that appeared after the flood of Noah in the Bible, she would never take that special bond and love for granted again.

I remember her interview like it was just yesterday:

"I lost that pin," Miss Ida B. had told me in her interview. "I felt so bad because my mother did change. It was as if that pin was symbolic. She lost her bitterness with life and spent the time she had with me. She was a kinder person. I wanted to pass the pin on to my children one day, but funny . . . I never had children. The last time I remember having the heart-shaped pin was at Rosedale because there were summers between college visits that I stayed with my mother there and helped her do day work as a maid. But I never found it. I looked all over." She sighed and shook her head from side to side.

CHAPTER 33

THE QUEEN OF HEARTS

Time does seem to move fast. As I get older, time seems as fast as light years. Every ticking second is the same measurement, but seconds lead into days and then years. I remember those playdates at the Rosedale House, and as I write the third and last book, I feel a sense of nostalgia and melancholy.

And our children grow up so fast. My daughter Michaela had just finished college and was moving out of our house into her own apartment. My husband and I spent the entire weekend moving all of her things. As I was setting up her bedroom with her, I noticed a beautiful and familiar piece of jewelry. It looked something like Miss Ida B.'s heart-shaped pin she had lost in the past. It was in Michaela's jewelry box. I picked it up and asked, "Hey, where did you buy this?"

"Oh, I never told you about this? It came from the Rosedale House. I found it in the garden one day while I was playing there. I asked Taylor's mom about it and she said I could keep it," Michaela chuckled. "It was not theirs. It was the same day we found the photographs and the red diary that belonged to Daisy. Remember that day? It was an exciting day. I'll never forget it."

I looked at it and smiled.

"You can have it, Mom. You always write about the Rosedale House and preserved its memory. I would like you to have it. Maybe the house does too." She smiled back and gave the pin to me. "From me to you with love!" She placed the pin on my lapel, "It's beautiful!"

I gasped because I knew the heart-shaped pin. It was always mine. It used to make me feel like a Queen. It was a souvenir of time travel. But I did not say anything because this was all too difficult to explain.

CHAPTER 34

AND THEN, I RISE

Crowds of tourists unload from large luxury buses and walk through the campus grounds. Other prospective students come and visit with their parents about the possibilities of future attendance. Nowadays, anyone can take a tour of the Princeton University campus and see Einstein's lecture hall.

Today, I visit Einstein's lecture hall again. It is a warm, sunny day and the glowing sun peers through the panes. I sit in the front seat of the first row in quiet. But in the quietness of the room, I hear a dripping sound. I look around the room to see where it may be coming from. Then, I feel a drop on my hand and another. I look up at the ceiling and smile. Then, I rise. I walk toward the door and exit, closing it behind me. And I remind my readers:

> One of the things we should understand about time is that we have just a little. Don't waste your time, humanity. You have just a little. It is the time traveler's secret.
>
> J. Richard Gott, *Time Travel in Einstein's Universe*

END NOTE

A LONG TALE: SYNCHRONICITY AND THE QUANTUM FIELD

Synchronicity is the door. The key is this moment in time. Time travel into the future and back again to the present takes place in the quantum field and consciousness of mind.

Imagine how those meetings of Jung and Einstein between 1905 and 1912 laid the foundation for synchronicity and time travel through the theories of relativity. In the quantum field, consciousness can travel at the speed of light from the future into present and from the past into the present by using Einstein's theories of relativity now supported by quantum mechanics. In synchronicity, consciousness, together with coincidence, masters a moment of travel into the past or future.

This scientific study of Jung, Einstein, and the quantum field at Princeton University led to my discovery of the possibility of time travel through synchronicity. Using this research, the literary, historical, and scientific construction of the final book of the series about Miss Ida B. came to be. The research helped to explain both the actual coincidences possible for time travel and the literary synchronicity connected with the writing of the Princeton series: *Quantum Leaps in Princeton's Place, Six Doors Down*, and *The Future Is My Past*.

In Jung's last book before his death in 1961, *Man and His Symbols*, one of his closest editors summarized the work and future work about Jung in this way:

> Creative ideas in my opinion show their value in that, like keys, they help to 'unlock' hitherto unintelligible connections of facts and thus enable man to penetrate deeper into the mystery of life. I am convinced that Jung's ideas can serve in this way to find and interpret new facts in many fields in science (and also of everyday life) simultaneously leading the individual to a more balanced, more ethical, and wider conscious outlook. If the reader should feel stimulated to work further on this investigation and assimilation of the unconscious—which always begins by working on oneself—the purpose of this introductory book would be fulfilled.

Thus, the foundation and explanation of another discovery: literary synchronicity about time travel in a trilogy about Princeton.

My abstract and scholarly paper about literary synchronicity and time travel in the quantum field was presented at the Center for Consciousness Studies—University of Arizona in Tuscon, Arizona for the April 2016 Conference and Poster Presentation entitled "*Quantum Leaps in Princeton's Plac*e on Synchronicity and the Quantum Field."

The Science of Consciousness (TSC) is the largest and

longest-running conference emphasizing broad and rigorous approaches to conscious awareness, the nature of existence, and our place in the universe. TSC brings together perspectives, orientations, and methodologies from neuroscience, philosophy, medicine, quantum physics, cosmology, biology, psychology, anthropology, artificial intelligence, technology, contemplative and experiential traditions, the arts, culture, humanities, and other disciplines.

AFTERWORD
TELESCOPES AND TIME MACHINES

Physicists and astronomers like to say "The telescope is a time machine." When we look farther into space, we see farther back into time. The Hubble telescope helps us to see objects that may have been in existence since the beginning of time. If an object is 2 billion light years away, we can see it as it looked 2 billion years ago. Quasars are the oldest and brightest objects of the universe. Quasars produce their energy and bright light from massive black holes with more energy than one hundred galaxies combined. A quasar is currently more than 13 billion light years away because the distance between us and it has been constantly stretching during the past 13 billion years.

Based on the research of seeing the past in the present and theories of quantum field, physicists continue to see time travel as a real possibility. And as time passes, this fourth dimension is relevant to the current events of the conscious observer.

The late physicist, Robert Dicke, the Albert Einstein Professor of Science Emeritus at Princeton University, explained the existence of our universe:

If you want an observer around, and if you want life, you need heavy elements. To make heavy elements out of hydrogen, you need thermonuclear combustion. To have thermonuclear combustion, you need a time of cooking in a star of several billion years. In order to stretch out several billion years in its time dimension, the universe, according to general relativity, must be several years across in its space dimensions. So why is the universe as big as it is? Because we are here!" (*Cosmic Search*, Vol. 1, No. 4, http://www.bigear.org/vol1no4/wheeler.htm)

Physicist Andrei Linde of Stanford University said, "The universe and the observer exist as a pair. I cannot imagine a consistent theory of the universe that ignores consciousness" (*Biocentrism: How Life and Consciousness Are the Keys to Understanding the Universe*).

And Stephen Hawking said, "The laws of science, as we know them at present, seem to have been very finely adjusted to make possible the development of life"

Fred Hoyle, in his book *Intelligent Universe*, compared "the chance of obtaining even a single functioning protein by a chance combination of amino acids to a star system full of blind men solving Rubik's Cube simultaneously"

In conclusion, "We are no longer satisfied with insights into particles, or fields of force, or geometry, or even space and time," Hoyle wrote in 1981. "Today we demand of physics some understanding of existence itself" (*The Voice of Genius: Conversations With Nobel Scientists and Other Luminaries*).

APPENDIX A
"ONE MOMENT IN TIME"

(Scholarly paper submitted to University of Arizona, Consciousness Studies, September 2017)

Synchronicity is about coincidence in single moments of time. In synchronicity, a moment unfolds the normal sequence of clock time. We experience extraordinary moments of timelessness through the experience of the conscious mind. Through my research and study at Princeton University, I discovered that synchronicity is the window, the key—this moment in time. Time travel into the future or past and back again to the present, takes place in the quantum field and consciousness of mind.

Synchronicity is quantum. In physics, the quantum field is the unifier of all consciousness.

Jung connected support from physics for his psychological theories. He confirmed that his work was influenced and connected by Einstein's theories of relativity in physics (1935, para. 140). His theories mimic aspects of Einstein's theory of relativity. Einstein's theory and the space-time continuum in physics are the sources from which Carl Jung derived the word *synchronicity* (1952b, para. 840).

Another way to think about synchronicity is the ability to distort time, arriving at a destination of thought by skipping steps. As a rupture in time, synchronicity transgresses the way time normally operates. Meaningful connection between events with no perceived a-causal connection. Time through this aspect of consciousness is therefore abolished, thereby making the present both the past and the future. The conscious is timeless.

And the novels *Quantum Leaps in Princeton's Place, Six Doors Down,* and *The Future is My Past* are written in a way that utilizes the theories of Carl G. Jung and Albert Einstein. Together, these theories suggest the possibilities of time travel into the future back into the present and the past back into the present through the quantum field of consciousness.

The creative trilogy of novels are framed by one of the four levels of inquiry into consciousness—Level 3: Depth-psychological Hermeneutics (Brian Lancaster, 2004). Specifically, this is representative of Jung's postulate of the collective unconscious. Mental and physical events are interrelated. Physical events can be intrinsically meaningful as in his concept of synchronicity. Depth psychology constructs and religion apply so that the concealed realm reveals itself through a series of meaningful events. Jung argued that this unseen unconscious contains archetypes that function to transmit knowledge to the conscious realm. Space and time are relative; knowledge finds itself in a space-time continuum that is no longer space or time (Jung, 1952b, para. 912).

It is similar to the existence of black holes in the universe. One can travel and find a shortcut to the other side through a rupture in time. As Jung noted, "I have established that it [synchronicity] closely resembles numinous experiences where space, time, and causality are abolished" (McGuire & Hull, 1978, p. 230).

APPENDIX B

CREATIVE WRITING AS A GESTURE IN SYNCHRONICITY

(Scholarly presentation and published paper at American University in Paris, France, June 14-16, 2017)

Synchronicity is serendipitous creativity. Moments in time when events come together to create product are art as gesture, in this case, the creative writing of my novel, *Six Doors Down*. The creative trilogy of the three novels are framed by one of the four levels of inquiry into consciousness—Level 3: Depth-psychological Hermeneutics (Lancaster, 2004).

Specifically, this is representative of Jung's postulate of the collective unconscious. Mental and physical events are interrelated. Physical events can be intrinsically meaningful as in his concept of synchronicity. Depth psychology constructs and religion apply so that the concealed realm reveals itself through a series of meaningful events. Jung argued that this unseen unconscious contains archetypes that function to transmit knowledge to the conscious realm. Space and time are relative; knowledge finds itself in a space-time continuum that is no longer space or time (Jung,

1952b, para. 912). Writing is an artistic gesture that captures the notion of synchronicity in the product as literature.

Synchronicity is about coincidence in single moments of time. In synchronicity, a moment unfolds the normal sequence of clock time. We experience extraordinary moments of timelessness through the experience of the conscious mind. Through my research and study at Princeton University, I discovered that synchronicity is the window, the key—this moment in time. Time travel into the future or past and back again to the present takes place in the quantum field and consciousness of mind.

Synchronicity is quantum. In physics, the quantum field is the unifier of all consciousness. Jung connected support from physics for his psychological theories. He confirmed that his work was influenced and connected by Einstein's theories of relativity in physics (1935, para. 140). His theories mimic aspects of Einstein's theory of relativity. Einstein's theory and the space-time continuum in physics are the sources from which Jung derived the word *synchronicity* (1952b, para. 840).

Another way to think about synchronicity is the ability to distort time, arriving at a destination of thought by skipping steps. As a rupture in time: Synchronicity transgresses the way time normally operates. Meaningful connection between events with no perceived a-causal connection. Time through this aspect of consciousness is therefore abolished, thereby making the present both the past and the future. The conscious is timeless.

And the novels *Quantum Leaps in Princeton's Place, Six Doors Down,* and *The Future is My Past* are written in a way that utilizes the theories of Carl G. Jung and Albert Einstein. Together, these theories suggest the possibilities of time travel into the future back into the present and the past back into the present through the quantum field of consciousness.

The documentation of this experience in synchronicity in creative writing is an artistic gesture of literature and creative work in the humanities. In other cases, the experiences are scientific documentations and writings such as the structure of the atom by Niels Bohr and the benzene ring molecule by August Kekule coming through the unconscious mind. Certainly, Jung believed in this power of consciousness in the human mind in the product of writing.

In Jung's last book before his death in 1961, *Man and His Symbols*, one of his closest editors summarized the work and future work of Jung in this way:

> Creative ideas, in my opinion show their value in that, like keys, they help to 'unlock' hitherto unintelligible connections of facts and thus enable man to penetrate deeper into the mystery of life. I am convinced that Jung's ideas can serve in this way to find and interpret new facts in many fields in science (and also of everyday life) simultaneously leading the individual to a more balanced, more ethical, and wider conscious outlook. If the reader should feel stimulated to work further on this investigation and assimilation of the unconscious—which always begins by working on oneself—the purpose of this introductory book would be fulfilled.

APPENDIX C
QUANTUM CONSCIOUSNESS AND POSSIBILITIES OF TIME TRAVEL

(Scholarly paper and presentation at Center for Consciousness Studies, University of Arizona, April 2018)

Physicists from Princeton University talked about that possibility of time travel through courses on Einstein and relativity. Time is a dimension of our existence. It was at that moment I thought of the meaning of Jung's synchronicity and the possibility of time travel. Jung also wrote about events taking place at a future time and being represented in the present time as synchronicity or meaningful coincidence (Jung, 1955, pp. 144-5).

When Einstein visited Zurich, Switzerland in 1909 and 1912, he often dined with Carl G. Jung, a Swiss psychologist and lecturer at Zurich University. Einstein's theories on relativity influenced the work of Jung. And so Jung wrote, "It was Einstein who started me off thinking about a possible relativity of time as well as space. . . . More than thirty years later this stimulus led to my relation with the physicist Professor W. Pauli and to my thesis on synchronicity" (1976, p. 109).

To Jung, space-time relativity was different. The conscious had similar qualities to quantum science. From Einstein's theory of relativity, Jung developed the definition of synchronicity as "conditioned relativity of space and time" (1952b, para. 840). He wrote about the timeless quality of the unconscious and space through quantum physics and also documented the influence of Albert Einstein in a letter:

> To Carl Seelig [Carl Seelig, the friend and first biographer (German-Swiss) of Albert Einstein]
>
> Dear Dr. Seelig, 25 February 1953
>
> I got to know Albert Einstein through one of his pupils, a Dr. Hopf if I remember correctly.
> Professor Einstein was my guest on several occasions at dinner, when, as you have heard, Adolf Keller was present on one of them and on others Professor Eugen Bleuler, a psychiatrist and my former chief.
> These were very early days when Einstein was developing his first theory of relativity.
> He tried to instill into us the elements of it, more or less successfully.
> As non-mathematicians we psychiatrists had difficulty in following his argument.
> Even so, I understood enough to form a powerful impression of him.
> It was above all the simplicity and directness of his genius as a thinker that impressed me

mightily and exerted a lasting influence on my own intellectual work.

It was Einstein who first started me off thinking about a possible relativity of time as well as space . . .

More than thirty years later this stimulus led to my relation with the physicist Professor W. Pauli and to my thesis of synchronicity.

With Einstein's departure from Zurich my relation with him ceased, and I hardly think he has any recollection of me.

One can scarcely imagine a greater contrast than that between the mathematical and the psychological mentality.

The one is extremely quantitative and the other just as extremely qualitative.

> With kind regards,
> Yours sincerely,
> C.G. Jung
> (Carl Jung, *Letters*, Vol. II, pp. 108-9, https://carljungdepthpsychology.wordpress.com/2015/08/02/how-dr-jung-met-albert-einstein/

The research of Einstein and Jung demonstrated a parallel between the psychology of synchronicity and the physics of time. These principles formed the foundation of time travel in *The Future Is My Past*. As Professor J. Richard Gott of the Astrophysics Department at Princeton University noted, "In the history of science, great breakthroughs often occur when someone realizes two situations thought to be different are actually the same or have a strong connection for further discovery."

The quantum process in the brain is capable of intertwining space and time (Buonomano, 2016, p. 193). And in my research and course study, synchronicity proves to be the window, the key—this moment in time. Time travel into the future and back again to the present takes place in the quantum field and consciousness of mind.

BIBLIOGRAPHY

Gott, J. R. (2001). *Time travel in Einstein's universe: The physical possibilities of travel through time*. New York, NY: Houghton Mifflin.

Herzog, M. H., Kammer, T., & Scharnowski, F. (2016??). Time slices: What is the duration of a percept? *PLoS Biology, 14*(4): e1002433. doi:10.1371/journal.pbio.1002433

James, W., & Nichida, K. (2007). *Pure experience, consciousness, and moral psychology*.

Jung, C. (1969). An acausal connecting principle. In *Collected Works, 8: The structure and the dynamics of the psyche* (2nd ed.). London, UK: Routledge and Kegan Paul.

Jung, C. (YEAR). *Carl Jung, Letters*, 2. Retrieved from

Lancaster, B. (2004). *Approaches to consciousness: The marriage of science and mysticism*. London, UK: Palgrave Macmillan.

McGuire, W., & Hull, R. F. C. (1978). *C. J. Jung speaking: Interviews and encounters*. London, UK: Thames and Hudson.

Main, R. (2004). *The rupture of time: Synchronicity and Jung's critique of modern Western culture.* London, UK: Routledge.

Ryden, B. (2010). *Foundations of astrophysics.* San Francisco, CA: Pearson.

APPENDIX D

ABSTRACT. TIME AS NOW. HERE AS SPACE: NEUROSCIENCE AND THEORY OF EINSTEIN RELATIVITY

Time has a special place of action called, the present. It is the dimension of our existence.

Everyone has 86,400 seconds of time for living every day. And all of our present moments become memories in the past with the passage of these seconds in time.

Time is also relative. Time can be illusion within the brain and consciousness. Warped senses of time exist due to focused attention and interest. One may watch the time on a clock for dismissal from a class and it seems to move slow. On other occasions, one can enjoy their time playing a sport and the time seems to move rapidly. The passage of time is a mental construct of the brain.

And the brain can serve as a time machine. The brain tells time. And time is part of the brain's operating system in its neurons and circuitry. The brain anticipates future events while operating in the present. The brain can act now to create a future when the future eventually becomes the present. And the brain's consciousness can also connect the present to the past.

Quantum events affect the states of the brain in time. Quantum processes of the brain exist in the field of neuroscience as they do in the outer field of physics. The inner workings of the brain must observe the outer world of physics. Physics is the structure of the world we live in.

In the quantum physics world, particles can exist in multiple points in space at once. The quantum world sets up the premise for time travel. Time travel as referred to in the trilogy of novels, is the marriage between neuroscience, psychology, consciousness, and physics.

Works Cited:

Hartle, James. *Gravity,* Benjamin-Cummings Publishing, 2002.

Schutz, Bernard. *A First Course in General Relativity,* Cambridge University Press, 2009.

APPENDIX E

ABSTRACT. QUANTUM CONSCIOUSNESS IN THE EXTREME

Abstract for Towards A Science of Consciousness, University of Arizona Conference, Tuscon, Arizona 2018

"In time-travel research, we are exploring extreme situations in which space and time are warped in unfamiliar ways." (Gott, 31) Space-time, the concepts of time and three-dimensional space are regarded as fused in a four-dimensional continuum. Mass tells space-time how to curve and space-time tells mass how to move.

In the same way, quantum physics disturbs our normal way of thinking about time in our reality, but proves to be true on the subatomic scale in physics. It is like *Alice in Wonderland*, objects may disappear and tunnel into another space in time or appear distorted and unexpected to the reality of the human eye.

Carl Jung and Albert Einstein laid the foundation for this notion in 1905-1912 with their discussion of synchronicity and physics. In the quantum field, consciousness can travel the speed of light from the future into the past and back into the present using Einstein's theory of relativity now supported by quantum mechanics.

My study of the field of astrophysics and the theory of relativity at Princeton University during the years of 2016-2018, helped me to connect the concepts of synchronicity together. The book, *The Future is My Past*, relies on this theory as part of the foundation for the book's premise in synchronicity and consciousness, the moment of coincidence that signifies the mastering of time travel.

Works Cited:

Bartusiak, Marcia. (2017) *Einstein's Unfinished Symphony: The Story of a Gamble, Two Black Holes, and a New Age of Astronomy.* Yale University Press, Connecticut

Chopra, Deepak. *Quantum Physics of Time.* Chopra Foundation, California, 2013.

Gott, J. Richard (2001). *Time Travel in Einstein's Universe: The Physical Possibilities of Travel Through Time.* New York, New York: Houghton Mifflin.

Halpern, Paul. (2017) *The Quantum Labyrinth: How Richard Feynman and John Wheeler Revolutionized Time and Reality*

Hartle, James. *Gravity,* Benjamin-Cummings Publishing, 2002.

Penrose, Sir Roger and Kak, Subhash (2012) *Quantum Physics of Consciousness,* Journal of Cosmology, Vol. 3 and 14, University of Oxford, London, England.

Schutz, Bernard. *A First Course in General Relativity,* Cambridge University Press, 2009.

ABOUT THE AUTHOR

Dr. Donna L. Clovis is a graduate of Columbia University in New York City in journalism and the humanities. She has won a first-place feature-writing award for the National Association of Black Journalists. Dr. Clovis has also won two journalism fellowships: the McCloy Fellowship from the American Council on Germany and Harvard University and a Prudential Fellowship from Columbia University. She is also the Albert Einstein Education Award winner for achievements that produce a significant improved educational environment from the governor of New Jersey.

She writes this book from Einstein's classroom and attends classes at Princeton University in theoretical physics in order to write about time travel in the last book of the trilogy.

Dr. Clovis is interested in documentary work and storytelling that comes from this type of journalism. This is the basis of her story and the synchronicity that occurred as she gathered the information through interviews and researching articles. It is called being in the right place at the right time. Dr. Clovis lives in the Princeton Junction area and loves to travel to other countries to learn more about people and culture.

IF YOU MISSED READING HER FIRST BOOK OF THE SERIES, *Quantum Leaps in Princeton's Place*...

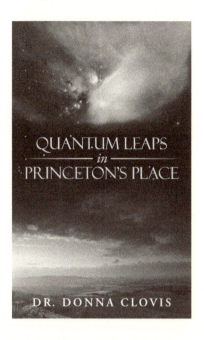

Award-winning journalist, Dr. Donna Clovis, recounts the stories of Princeton, New Jersey, in the early 1900s through the late 1950s through the eyes of two of the oldest citizens by means of interviews, diaries, and articles. The synchronicity of being at the right place at the right time for the interviews, locations, and journals plays a major role in the construction of the book.

CONTACT:

Dr. Donna Clovis invites conversation about her books through Facebook Dakota Clovis, named after her companion Golden Retriever and quantumclovis@gmail.com. Follow Dr. Clovis on Twitter @clovid01 and on her writing blog: donnaclovis.blog.